D1608361

Mishka
An Adoption Tale

Mishka
An Adoption Tale

Written by Adrienne Ehlert Bashista
Illustrated by Miranda R. Mueller

drt press

Thanks to Mark, Jacob, and Jamie – my own forever family!

— Adrienne

I would like to thank my Grandma for all her love and patience during the many hours I spent drawing in her leaky attic, my Mama for believing in a little girl's dream of becoming a children's book illustrator, and of course my darling Amber for being the sweetest and most beautiful pup that could ever inspire an artist to draw animals.

—Miranda

Text copyright © 2007 by Adrienne Ehlert Bashista.
Illustrations copyright © 2007 by Miranda R. Mueller.

Cover and interior text design and layout by Stephen Tiano, Book Designer & Page Composition Specialist

For more information about DRT Press and books on adoption and families, please see www.drtpress.com or write to us at DRT Press, P.O. Box 427, Pittsboro, NC 27312.

First edition.

The illustrations in the book were done in pastel and prismacolor on Artagain paper.

Printed in China.

Publisher's Cataloging-in-Publication Data

Bashista, Adrienne Ehlert.
    Mishka : an adoption tale / by Adrienne Ehlert Bashista ; illustrated by Miranda R. Mueller.
    p. cm.
    ISBN 978-1-933084-01-5
[1. Intercountry adoption--Fiction. 2. Adoption--Fiction. 3. Teddy bears--Fiction.] I. Mueller, Miranda R. II. Title.

PZ7.B2917 M57 2007
[E]--dc22   2007923998

This book is for my son Jamie, my real-life Yuri, and for the thousands of other children adopted from Russia and Eastern Europe each year. It's also for the hundreds of thousands, if not millions, of children in orphanages all over the world, in the hopes that someday they will meet the family of their dreams.

—Adrienne Ehlert Bashista

Mo sat high on a shelf in an airport gift shop.

Every day he watched as people rushed by. He wondered where they were going, and what they were like. Often, he'd see a mother and a father and some children and he'd long for them to come into the shop and buy him, but no one ever did.

More than anything, Mo wanted a family. He wanted a home.

One day a man and a woman came into the store.
Mo watched them as they picked up one thing, then another.
"I want something special," the woman said.
"How about this?" the man asked, wrapping his warm hands around
Mo's belly.
"Perfect," the woman said.
Mo knew his family had found him.

On the airplane, Mo sat snug between the man and the woman. He was excited to belong to someone, but he had so many questions. "Where are we going?" he thought. "Are we going home?"

He imagined his new home. He hoped there would be children, and lots of fun. One of the children might sleep with him at night! Mo could hardly wait.

After the plane landed, they went outside. A girl poked Mo's chubby side. "Mishka," she said.

"What's a mishka?" Mo wondered. He shivered. The air smelled different here. "Where are we?" he thought. "Is this my home?"

Their taxi brought them to a big city. The people on the streets walked quickly, holding their coats tight against the cold wind.

Finally, they stopped in front of a squat, grey building and went inside. "I can't wait to see him," the woman said.

"See who?" Mo thought.

Then the door opened.

A doctor came in, tugging a little boy by the hand.
"Mama," the doctor said, pointing to the woman.
"Papa," the doctor said, pointing to the man.
"Yuri," the doctor said, and pointed to the little boy.
The little boy frowned. He looked at the ground.

"Yuri," the woman said. "I brought you something."

"I am a gift," thought Mo. "For a little boy!"

Yuri looked up. "Mishka," he whispered.

The man, the woman, Yuri, and Mo played all afternoon. They couldn't understand each other, but that didn't seem to matter.

They played catch, using Mo as a ball.

They slid down the slides in the playground outside Yuri's building.

They drew pictures with crayons the woman had in her purse.

By the end of the day they were all friends.
"This is my family," Mo thought, and he was happy.

Then the doctor came back. She took Yuri's hand.

"We have to leave now," the woman said.

Mo was confused. "Where were they going?" he thought.

Yuri tried to hand Mo to the woman.

"No, no, Yuri," she said. "You keep him. He'll be a reminder of us"

"That's right," said the man. "Before you know it we'll be back to take you home."

"Home," Yuri repeated, but Mo could tell he didn't understand.

"Take us now!" Mo wanted to yell, but he was made of stuffing and had no words.

That night, they slept in a room with a dozen other children. Snug under Yuri's arm, Mo heard the little boy whisper, "Mishka…Mama…Papa."

Mo missed the man and the woman. He hoped that they would come back. He wanted them to take him and Yuri home.

The next morning, Yuri and Mo sat with the other children at square tables. "Po-esht, mishka," Yuri said, lifting a spoon filled with porridge to Mo's mouth.

Later, they listened to music. "Tah-nets, mishka," Yuri said, dancing Mo around the room.

That night when they lay in their bed, Yuri tucked the covers around Mo's shoulders. "Saun, mishka," he said softly.

Days went by, each day much the same as the last. Every morning there was porridge, every afternoon was music, and every night was the bed in the room filled with a dozen other sleeping children.

Mo thought his new life with Yuri was much better than his life on the gift shop shelf. He loved it when they played together.

But he wondered if the man and the woman were ever going to return. It had been a long time since they'd left.

Finally, when the leaves started to appear on the trees outside Yuri's window, the man and the woman came back.

Yuri's eyes lit up when he saw them, but he was quiet. Mo could tell he felt shy.

"We've come to take you home," said the man.

Yuri still didn't say anything, but held out Mo for the man and the woman to see.

"This bear is dirty!" the woman said, laughing. "He needs a bath." She hugged Yuri and Mo anyway. "I am so happy to see you," she said. "I missed you more than you will ever know."

"Mama," whispered Yuri, while the woman was hugging him, and Mo knew that everything would be all right.

Then it was time for the man and the woman to leave again, but now Yuri and Mo would be going with them.

"Pa-ka, Yura!' the caretakers said. "Pa-ka, mishka!" So long!

Yuri held onto Mo with one hand and the woman's hand with the other. "Pa-ka!" he yelled back. "Dos Vee-dan-ya!"

Their taxi drove through the big city. Mo felt Yuri's heart pound. The little boy's eyes darted this way and that. He didn't say a word.

Yuri held Mo tighter than he'd ever been held before.

Their taxi stopped. They got out. "We are going into the Embassy now," the man said. "This is where they give us the papers that will let us take you home."

They entered a room full of people. Babies, children, men and women all filled the chairs lining the edges of the room.

Every once in a while a name was called and some of the people went to a window. The woman behind the window gave them a thick envelope and then the people left.

They found three chairs of their own. The woman
gave Yuri some crackers.

"Po-esht, mishka," Yuri said, holding a cracker to
Mo's mouth, then to his own.

"Po-esht means eat, I think," the man said. "I wonder
what 'mishka' means."

After all this time, Mo thought he knew.

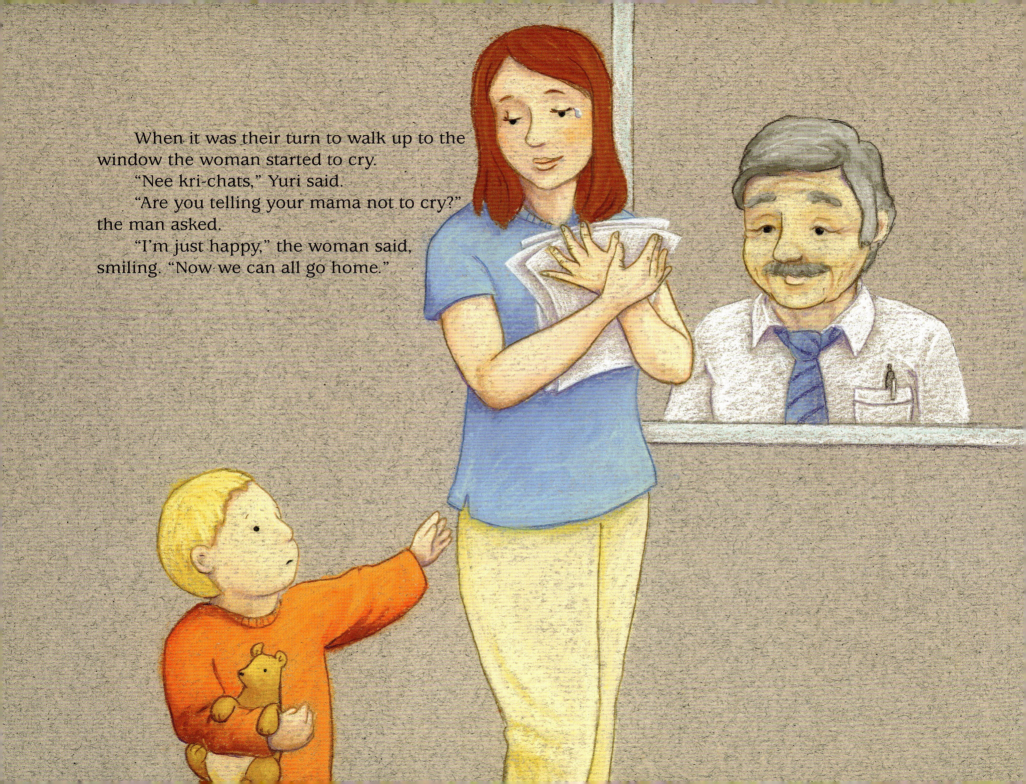

When it was their turn to walk up to the window the woman started to cry.

"Nee kri-chats," Yuri said.

"Are you telling your mama not to cry?" the man asked.

"I'm just happy," the woman said, smiling. "Now we can all go home."

That night they boarded a plane. "Sit here, Yuri," the man said. "See-dee-tee," he read out of a book.

Yuri smiled and sat down between the man and the woman. "See-dee-tee, mishka," he said. He tucked Mo next to him.

"There's that word," the man said. "Mishka." He looked in the book again "Oh! Mishka means bear. Little bear." He poked Mo in the belly. "Mishka."

"Mishka. That's me," thought Mo. "And I'm right where I belong."

For more information about DRT Press and books on adoption and families, please see www.drtpress.com or write to us at:
DRT Press
P.O. Box 427
Pittsboro, NC 27312

DRT Press is proud to give 5% of all profits to organizations serving the children of the world.

To learn more about adoption from Russia, please contact Families of Russian and Ukranian Adoption (FRUA) through their website: www.frua.org
And Eastern European Adoption Coalition (EEAC) at www.eeadopt.org

To all the children who have become new friends with Bear.
Thank you for reading my books!
– K. W.

For Boo – I love you.
– J. C.

SIMON AND SCHUSTER
First published in Great Britain in 2006 by Simon & Schuster UK Ltd
Africa House, 64-78 Kingsway, London WC2B 6AH
A CBS COMPANY

Originally published in 2006 by Margaret K. McElderry Books,
an imprint of Simon & Schuster Children's Publishing Division, New York

The text for this book is set in Adobe Caslon
The illustrations are rendered in acrylic paint

A CIP catalogue record for this book is available from the British Library upon request

ISBN 1 416 91739 X
EAN 9781416917397

Printed in China

1 3 5 7 9 10 8 6 4 2

SIMON AND SCHUSTER

First published in Great Britain in 2006 by Simon & Schuster UK Ltd
Africa House, 64–78 Kingsway, London WC2B 6AH
A CBS COMPANY

Originally published in 2006 by Margaret K. McElderry Books,
an imprint of Simon & Schuster Children's Publishing Division, New York

The text for this book is set in Adobe Caslon
The illustrations are rendered in acrylic paint

A CIP catalogue record for this book is available from the British Library upon request

ISBN 1 416 91739 X
EAN 9781416917397

Printed in China

1 3 5 7 9 10 8 6 4 2

To all the children who have become new friends with Bear.
Thank you for reading my books!
– K. W.

For Boo – I love you.
– J. C.

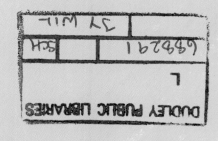